DAMIA WILLIS, F.B.I
Faith Bureau of Investigations

Copyright © 2015, C.KQ. LLC
www.ckqllc.biz/getpublished.html

'Damia Willis/Golden Lady' designed by Denzel Henderson

ISBN-10: 0988229374
ISBN-13: 978-0-9882293-7-2

Damia Willis, F.B.I. is an intriguing work of Christian fiction that pulls you in from the very beginning, keeps you in suspense until the end and leaves you salivating for more! The author, Dana Neal, did a wonderful job of crafting Damia's character to be relatable; she is strong, yet not afraid to acknowledge her weaknesses. She's a woman passionate about her life's mission and is willing to do whatever it takes to see it come to fruition! Damia's faith teaches us about having unwavering faith in GOD, even when we don't understand His plan.

Shamico Winger

I truly enjoyed the book. I couldn't stop reading. I love suspense. It was well written, very engaging. When is Book 2 coming? Great story!

Alba Henderson

Table of Contents

CHAPTER 1:
THE WEEKEND

Matthew 22:14 (NKJV)
For many are called, but few are chosen

They left the building with bags in tow. Ronesha Smith was behind them all the way, hustling and bustling to get things going. Damia Scott, and Anthony Bishoff, were about to take their friendship to another level that was not in the plans some 12 years ago. The look on Anthony's face was one of disbelief; He was leaving the life he once knew.

It was Monday morning; the staff hadn't come in yet, and answering questions was not what they wanted to do. It was a shock to them what was happening, but they couldn't wait on what next or ponder what next, it was time to go. The emotions that had come over them in the brief 24 hours to make this decision were those of intensity, fear, anxiety, and confusion. The last five days weren't a walk in the park either; all of them knew that this had to be done in order to save and help the masses. It was January 2015, and their worlds were changing. It was last Monday that seemed to set the ball rolling:

Damia was in her office feeling oddly tired after lunch. She brushed it off as the 'itis' from having such a full meal. Damia decided to get her favorite beverage from the break room. As she walked in that direction, she noticed no one was where they should be; not Ronesha, Anthony, and curiously, not the receptionist. Damia started to get a strange feeling that she couldn't shake. The lighting in the room got dim and the air thin. Damia approached the break room to see Anthony and Ronesha standing there talking. As Damia stepped in, she noticed they didn't hear nor see her, but she could hear them. It was at this point she knew she was dreaming; whether at home or at work, she was dreaming.

"She's got to go do what God has called her to do," Anthony was saying to Ronesha

"I understand that," She replied, "but why should we suffer? What will we do once she's gone? Who will train whom?" Ronesha seemed very concerned about the office. Damia felt like she walked into a conversation God meant for her to hear.

"Our issues are not her problem," Anthony went on, "but if we don't let her go and tell her we know she should go, then we will have more problems than not."

Damia heard her name being called and she turned to answer, as she turned she woke up in her office. It *was Ronesha trying to get her attention.*

"Are you okay?" She asked. Feeling embarrassed for being sleep, Damia nodded her head and yawned. "Well, good; I need you to look over these real estate contracts you sent out last week and sign the fax cover sheets that you sent them out. The main office is really hounding down on verification." Ronesha rolled her eyes noting that the verification was not that vital to the completion of the entire task.

Damia smiled and said, "Signing the fax verification isn't the proof they should be looking for, but I'll sign." As lead consultant for real estate properties with the City of Milwaukee, Damia had a work ethic that saved the office from a great despair; in a nut shell, she kept them from falling on their butts!

It was 3:30 pm and almost time to go. She realized that the dream she had was longer than she thought, and was still lingering in her mind. She left the office ready to tackle the things of home. As she got in her truck, she looked at the Cadillac Escalade EXT and recalled how God showed this vehicle to her in visions. How He reminded her that it was hers so many times, now that she was driving it, in the bitter cold and snow, she thought about the rough past year, of moving out of her home and leaving her husband; in just two days the divorce will be final.

Two days after the dream day, Damia was on her way to work when Ronesha called her cell phone. This was quite odd, considering both of them would see each other shortly.

"How far from the office are you?" Ronesha asked.

"About 10 minutes; give or take. Why?" Damia answered, knowing the snow may slow her down.

"I need you to meet me at the front door before you go in," Ronesha replied.

"Okay; is everything okay?" Damia always worried about others, and never regarded a request as normal.

"Yes." Ronesha hung up before Damia could call her a liar.

As she walked to the front of the building, Damia looked around and realized how the city had changed so much; how things looked very different to her, the now almost single lead office assistant. Damia laughed as she shook her head remembering the last few years or her marriage.

"What are you laughing at?" Anthony Bishoff was walking up to the entrance looking at her as if

was annoyed that she was laughing.

"Oh, the memories of my marriage; you know today is the day the judge signs on the dotted line. Today is the day the ink dries immediately." Damia answered.

"Whatever," He said which caused Damia to laugh more; she recalled the times she cried in her office about the situation.

As he went in the building onto the elevator, Ronesha walked up slowly. Damia took in Ronesha's posture, and braced herself for whatever was going to come out of her mouth.

"Well, yesterday after you left the office, Anthony and I had a little meeting. We talked about your spirituality and how it affects the office," Ronesha looked at Damia waiting on any response. Damia was taken aback, but there wasn't enough information to snap out on, "We know that you are a great benefit to us, but we also know, from things you have shared with us, that God is calling you to something greater; something that will benefit the world at large."

"Um, okay," was all that Damia could muster up in an answer, "I'm almost afraid to ask what else."

"Well, what else is this," Ronesha got a real supervisory look on her face, "you have to decide today what to do; as a matter of fact, tomorrow morning, you need to make a decision. I know in my heart of hearts, that if you don't have an answer from God, an answer will be made for you. After the meeting, after I was at home, I could hear God say, it won't be long. I knew it had to do with you. This morning, on my way to work, I heard Thursday." Damia noticed a change in Ronesha's posture; she started to slump as if to know the answer was already there. Her eyes started to glaze over as well, and *she looked like she wanted to go home.*

"Ronesha, this is a lot to take in because I didn't realize you and Anthony had such a spiritual connection that you do; God has spoken through you and I have to take it to prayer and see what He wants me to do next. Yes, I feel like the answer is already there," she put her hand on Ronesha's shoulder as she continued; "I love my job. I have never wanted leave you guys unless the Lord says so. At this point, I must get ready."

Ronesha looked Damia deep in her eyes, with buckets of tears rolling down her face and said, "There is more that is going to happen and it will affect the office, and your life, but I can't even tell you what that is until you talk to us tomorrow." Ronesha hugged Damia tight and then walked in the building.

After the divorce proceedings, Damia went home, had dinner, and got into her prayer closet to talk with God about all that had happened that day. She was no longer Mrs. but Ms and now needed to ask God about how to leave the job. The conversation she had with Ronesha was confirmation of what God had been saying for years. It was also confirmation of the dream she had while at work earlier this week.

Thursday morning came so quickly, Damia felt she had just closed her eyes. She remembered the dream she had and knew what to do when she got to the office. As she looked around her room, she was glad that all of her children were grown, and wouldn't have to give her a hard time about quitting, she also knew that her trying to put in two weeks notice easily was going to be hard on everyone. Yet, she couldn't help but wonder what else Ronesha knew.

While in the shower, Damia heard a 'commotion' in her hallway. Her daughter Qu'ilasia was out of town and no one else had a key. 'Well, that would be a lie,' she thought, 'my husband still has a key.' She opened the door to the bathroom and saw nothing in the hallway, but it was what was on the floor that startled her.

"Now how in the world did that get there?" Damia said aloud. It was her passport and travel codes for her travel business. Just then a slight wind blew in her hallway and she was hearing someone say 'GO'. Damia was no stranger to spiritual encounters so she was not afraid; at this point, she was trying to find luggage and think of something to say at work.

Damia got to work during the rush hour traffic without haste, and quickly got to her office before anyone came in. It was 6:45 in the morning, she had to start the coffee and pack some personal items as *she was spiritually aware that things were about to hit the fan and change a lot faster than a simple two week notice. At 7:15 Anthony and Ronesha walked into Damia's office with boxes in hand. They closed the door behind them, looked at Damia and almost started talking at once.*

"We have to get this stuff packed up." Anthony said. He started to get everything that was personal to Damia off of shelves and closets and into boxes. Damia was in shock, because she hadn't said she was leaving.

Almost reading her mind, Ronesha said, "We know you're going to do what is right. We know you are putting your notice in today. I typed up the resignation letter; all you have to do is sign it. Your things are not going to your house; we're putting them in storage just in case you ever have to come back."

Damia's mouth dropped. Everything had been done for her. She felt like she was being pushed out, but in her spirit she knew there was something she was missing. Visions of her dream came rushing back to her like waves of water that she swayed right into her desk chair. She could hear the Lord say F.B.I., and various other instructions. Damia was losing her footing and sliding out of the chair when Anthony caught her and presented her with a small, empty brown box.

"You have to remember whatever it is that has you loopy. You have to write it down. Then I want you to put it and every other note you have in your purse and your desk in this box. I'm not even sure why I'm asking you to do this, but it was something I dreamed about on Monday." 'Monday, Damia thought, that was the day I had the dream during lunch.' Anthony went on to say, "you have to go do whatever God wants you to do.

You can't keep holding back. We'll be fine here; you do what you have to do."

"Damia," Ronesha interjected, "Write down what you remember from last night."

And she did; she wrote down everything, she put it in the bottom of the box and filled the box with every note, every instruction, even thing she had from God in her purse or desk. By the time she was done, Ronesha and Anthony had explained to the staff that Damia was leaving and that it would be two weeks or less. The main office had been contacted before Damia even got to the office that day. They had a plan for a catered lunch, and then to train the receptionist briefly on Damia's duties.

On Friday morning, there was a gold envelope with a gold seal on it addressed to Damia Willis. "That's funny, my last name is still Scott;

who would know my, or even, use my maiden name?" Damia thought out loud. As she opened the envelope, anything she might have forgotten from her dream the other day, was rushing back. This letter was a notice from the government in Nassau, Bahamas, specifically Paradise Island, informing Damia that everything was in order. Before she could even understand this fully, all hell broke loose in the office. The department head from man office was in Anthony's office trying to fight for Damia to stay. Ronesha ran in his office and shut the door; they stayed there for hours. At the end of the day the chief of police stopped by, handed Damia another gold envelope, saluted her, and went into Anthony's office, and again, CLOSED THE DOOR. He was a good friend to the staff, but too much was happening that she didn't understand, but at this point there was nothing she could do. Monday would bring some *answers. She threw the envelope in her purse, and left for the weekend.*

Sunday afternoon, as Damia got ready for a new work week, her doorbell rang. She wasn't expecting anyone, and Qu'ilasia was not back yet. It was her condo manager, Anthony and Ronesha. Another shock because they had never been to her house, and the unexpected visit on a Sunday was mind-blowing.

"Damia," Ronesha started, "We've paid off your lease. Qu'ilasia will stay here another month until Eugene can pick her up or she'll stay with one of your other children. I'm trying really hard here not to over step my bounds, but can you please fill in the blanks here?"

"What blanks? I'm following your lead!" Damia said looking at Ronesha and Anthony, "I'm not sure what to say do. I just know whatever it is its spiritual. I can't

remember much from the night I prayed, but every time I want to go in a normal direction you guys come rushing out of nowhere. AND WHAT DO YOU MEAN YOU PAID OFF MY LEASE?"

Anthony laughed an uneasy laugh, but started to tell what sounded like a short version of a long story, "On Monday, someone visited us after you left the office. This man said you were going to have to go, which is something we understood for a long time, but he said you would have to go, and things in our lives would be turned upside down." Anthony paused and looked at Ronesha while the condo manager surveyed the unit.

"Well, all is well." The manager said and walked towards the door, "The security deposit will be sent to the new address you gave." He said to Anthony.

"What new address?" Damia stated, "What is going on?"

"Well," Anthony continued, "the man also said I had to go with you." Damia gave him one of those looks like explain quickly, "Yes, it was a shock to me as well." He started pacing the floor when Ronesha spoke up.

"Look we're not sure what's happening, but only you know fully, Damia. Whether it's clear now or its clear later only you know. The man told us what to do for the days following. That's why I spoke to you in front of the building the other day, and why it seems like things are being unraveled at the office. No one wants you to go; those that don't understand. But," Ronesha hesitated.

"But, what? What else is there?" Damia asked.

"They don't know Anthony is leaving too. As soon as both of you leave the office, all the instructions

God gave you will start to fall into place. You will feel like you did years ago, when you didn't understand every thing, but you had to act on what you knew," Ronesha's eyes got distant as if she wasn't there, "You will have to take both gold envelops with you and put them in the box. It's going to be the box of secrets until a later time. Did you open the envelope from the chief?"

Damia got the envelope from her purse and read it aloud:

'Damia Willis is hereby appointed to be head agent of the newly established section of the F.B.I entitled F.B.I: Faith Bureau of Investigations. She has all licenses, certifications, and qualifications needed to run this bureau, as well as credentials to hire and establish worldwide locations. Colonel Anthony Bishoff will be her supervisory aide. He will adhere to her instructions and lead, but will be her security and protector as

specified in the directives given to him.'

Damia looked up from reading the note and some thing came over her. Something she hadn't felt in a long time; the feeling of surety, confidence, and anxiousness to get on assignment. "I'll pack." She said point blank, "Are you packed, Anthony?"

"Yes." He said matter of factly, "I've been packed since Tuesday."
"Ronesha, we'll need a ride to the airport. I have a feeling Friday was our last day." Ronesha nodded her head pulled a folder of papers from her purse, and handed them to Damia.

"Don't look at these until tomorrow morning. Someone will be here when you get ready to leave to drive you to the office. Love you girl." She hugged Damia and walked out the house.

Anthony lingered for a few seconds and put his hand on Damia's shoulder saying, "I'm not sure why they chose me, but after all we've been through in the past few years, I'm honored to serve you."

Through the night, visions, dreams and conversations with the Lord went on and on. Damia wrote note after note and put it in the box. She remembered hearing pack light, so when she woke up Monday morning, she packed 5 outfits for a week, her bibles, note cards and markers. She was ready; no turning back.

CHAPTER 2:
NO LOOKING BACK

Matthew 8:19(NKJV)
*Then a certain scribe came and said to
Him, "Teacher, I will follow You
wherever You go."*

In the backseat of the car,
Damia was still trying to
remember what the Lord said
over the weekend and making
sure she was walking in
everything that was asked of
her. They all walked into the
office that morning leaving all
work identification, keys, and
important procedures on
Ronesha's desk, and were out
the door before anyone could
see them. Damia couldn't
understand how Anthony was
totally involved in this, but for
some reason he had an idea,
and Ronesha was ready to take
over the office. Some things had
changed in 3 days that
catapulted Damia's spirituality

and Ronesha and Anthony's understanding into something greater. There were strangely magnificent things going on, but not that Damia could explain them all.

Just that second she remembered the Lord said burry the box in the back of the house she still owned with her husband.

"Ronesha go to my house on 71st street first. I know it is out of the way, but I we have to bury this box." As they got closer to the house, Damia didn't realize how high on a hill the house was; it seemed steeper than it had been in the past. The house was empty. Eugene wasn't staying there much and the kids didn't want to live there. With a since of nostalgia, Damia knew that this house would never be the same.

Back in the car, Anthony driving this time, Damia opened the folder full of papers that Ronesha had given her the previous day. On top was the outline of the teaching Damia had created a year earlier; Prophetic Patterns. The class hadn't gone as Damia expected, but she couldn't turn away from what she was called to do. Either way this outline was something that she had tossed so many months ago.

"Who was the man that came to see you two? What was his name? What did he look like?" Damia asked.

"He was just an average Joe; very polite, but new you well," Ronesha answered, "Why do you ask?"

"I threw these papers out last year when I started the teaching and finished the book. There isn't any way someone could have pulled these out of the garbage all nice and neat; even has my highlights on it."

"If we can call him Joe, he said that in this envelop you will find reminders that will stir up your prophetic gifting and your spiritual calling. These papers will help you develop the F.B.I. that will help Christians prepare fully for the rapture." This is what Damia was dreading to say at that point; honestly admitting that the preparation for the end was more imminent now; the people would have to choose the Lord or not.

As they approached the airport, Ronesha started crying out loud. In her face were the reluctance and the relief she had been holding back for days. Before they made it to the ticket desk they saw a man holding a gold sign with their names on it.

"The reason why Anthony is going is because he's going to protect you. His spiritually illogical mind will help your spiritual logical responses. There is no other way to do this PROPERLY than to send him with you. He's going increase in his spirituality as the years go on, but right now, his assignment is YOU."

"Ok." Damia said.

Anthony and Ronesha turned to her and said in unison, "Okay what?"

"One of you just explained why Anthony is going with me; full conversation just happened here." They looked at her strangely and shook their heads, and kept walking towards the man with the sign.

With an island accent, the man heartily greeted them, taking their bags, and said, "Hello!! I am Michael. I am so happy to serve you both in your travels. I will be taking you to your boarding area and will wait with you until your plane leaves. My instructions were to make sure the plane got in the air. You will be flying first class to Nassau Bahamas. Another man with a gold sign will be there waiting for you, and further instructions will be given." He put the bags on the cart and continued speaking as if speaking to Ronesha only, saying, "Here is where we must part; the assignments have begun however long it takes. Good byes come with sweet sorrow. I am proud to have served you this far Agent Willis and Colonel Bishoff. May God continue to lead you."

Ronesha turned to us and smiled. Damia remembered when they hired her to work in that office. She remembered the friendships; more like the family connection they all made. The past few days had literally brought them closer together; so close in their personal spaces that there was no turning back. Damia smiled as she thought to herself: *I'm thankful God chose them to be my co-laborers.*

As Ronesha started to speak her voice broke, and the tears started to flow again, "I'm not sure I'm ready for all that is about to happen and I don't know if I'll ever be ready. Only God knows the time Jesus will come back, but what I know right now, is that if He is putting you in place to help others until He gets back, we

33

must take heed to that! So even though I'll cry my heart out later, I'm ready to let you both go." She looked directly at Anthony and said, "You make sure nothing happens to either of you, but you BETTER FULLY MAKE SURE that nothing happens to Damia; she's on assignment."

"Alright, Boss." Anthony smiled at Ronesha and hugged her.

"No matter where we are," Damia started, "We're only a phone call away. Make sure you have your passport ready, okay? When you get back to the office, tell Adam I'm sorry, but it's necessary. I'm sure he'll understand why." Ronesha hugged her as she said "Okay." Anthony and Damia walked to the boarding gate to start on this new level of life.

Oddly enough, they never did talk about the voice Damia heard explaining why Anthony was going, too.

CHAPTER 3:
A NEW BEGINNING

Ephesians 4:3 NKJV
*Endeavoring to keep the unity of the spirit
in the bond of peace*

Two months had passed since
Anthony and Damia arrived in
the Bahamas. Their permanent
living quarters were on
Paradise Island, but far apart
from each other in order not to
become dependant. In order to
get to them, and where they
lived, someone had to go
through the main office in
Nassau. This was an office that
even Damia and Anthony knew
nothing about; the location as
well as their housing was secret
to outside individuals.

Anthony had gone through
some extensive training with a
private security firm to learn
how to shoot, how to see but
not be seen and how to leave
his emotions out of certain

circumstances. His training also consisted of him working under cover with the CIA. Damia was unaware of what the undercover work entailed, but she knew God knew.

Damia's training, or preparation, was more spiritual than anyone would have thought. She was taken to a hotel hidden away on one of the islands, where she met a minister that had been a pivotal part of her life, in the past, and she didn't know.

Minister L.A. Dallas was not what she expected. He was very manner able and articulate in the Bible. He had an anointing about him that caused you to think using what God gave you, instead of you pulling on him. Damia was not ready for all that she had gone through. She still felt residual of her 'training' and couldn't pull it all together.

On March 16, 2015, Damia woke up in her luxurious apartment with a knot in her stomach that threw her back on her pillows. She could hear conversations in her head, and then all of sudden she started speaking in spiritual tongues. It was so overwhelming that she wanted to cry and sleep all at the same time. Damia moaned aloud as the tongues subsided. She felt weak. The knock at her bedroom door brought her back to the realization that she would never be alone again; someone would always be there.

"Ma'am, are you okay? Agent Wills," The maid, Stephanie, called out almost in a panic, "Are you okay?"

"Yes," Damia answered; although she felt like that was a lie, "I'm just getting up."

"Colonel Bishoff has called you twice this morning, ma'am, and your driver is waiting for you."

Driver? Damia thought. *I can't get used to this.* She got up and took a shower; she noticed it was already 11:00. *My word, I'm late.*

As Damia went into the kitchen, Stephanie smiled at her and said, "You're the boss, technically, so you're not late. Your breakfast is in your office and the driver is still waiting."

As she walked in her office, she realized all the detail in everything in her apartment. It was Victorian and modern, as well as, a fortress for her protection. Her driver was the man that met her and Anthony at the airport two months ago. Funny; his name was Antonio.

"Agent Willis, good morning," Antonio said, standing as she came in the room, "How are you feeling today?"

"I'm feeling fine. Not used to being late, but according to Stephanie, I'm the boss." Damia laughed as she started to eat her breakfast. She motioned for him to sit down and asked, "What's up?"

Lifting an eyebrow at her form of the question, Antonio answered, "We must get you and Colonel Bishoff acclimated the first day at the office. There will not be any fan fair as you may say, but we will need to get things going, as there are people who need you, right now. I am not only your driver, but also your personal security."

Damia looked up from her food and studied his face for a short time. *Security?* She thought to herself.

Information started to flood her memory; the paperwork from the day they left Milwaukee had specific instructions. As she got up to look for them, and take her plate to the kitchen, Antonio called out to Stephanie, "Please come and retrieve this plate for Agent Willis. We're headed to the F.B.I.," He looked over at Damia and held out a gold trench coat, "The papers are already at the office; Colonel Bishoff is waiting for us. We must be going."

Anthony was in the lobby of her building; they hadn't seen each other for two months. When Anthony looked up and saw Damia and Antonio approaching, he smiled and reached out to hug her.

"Good morning, Agent Willis," He whispered in her ear, "This is really strange." He pulled back and headed towards the car.

"You have a file in the car you need to go over before we get to the office." Antonio stated as they got in the car.

Settling in her seat, Damia grabbed the file, in which, Anthony took it from her. "What are you doing?" She said, ready to snatch it back.

"According to my training, you're the boss, but I'm the regulator." He never looked up from the file.

Damia just rolled her eyes. She was trying to enjoy the scenery but her mind kept filling with different conversations she had with Minister Dallas. She shook it off and looked back at Anthony. "Is your apartment in my building?"

Never looking up he answered, "Yes. I'm one floor below you, but you realize our 'apartments' are one entire floor each, right?" She laughed and nodded her head. It was so funny to go from middle income living in Milwaukee, to wealth and riches in the Bahamas.

As she looked out the window again, she remembered how she and Eugene had been here once so many years ago. Things had obviously changed; a decade had past actually. Damia was glad to be here, but there were still some things that weren't clear; like, WHY HERE? All these thoughts went through her head.

"This file is telling us the specifics of our duties," Anthony's voice interrupted her thoughts; "I thought we already knew this? Wait, here is the small print: we can't tell anyone what we actually do."

"Anthony, we're good at that. We know how to keep people out of our business." Damia continued to look out the window, "How do you explain to the general public that we're not preachers and pastors, but a new breed of leaders helping the saints make it? How do you explain to people that God will show me what is necessary to help them out, and that we just SHOW UP? Really? I'm sure you thought about that for the past two months. "

He looked at her and just mouthed *SHUT UP*. They both laughed and tried to shake the strangeness that was starting to envelop the back of the vehicle.

Suddenly, Damia was not in the limo, she was in the garden at Minister Dallas' home. He was holding her hand and looking at her like a father would a child. She felt at ease in the garden, and, oddly, in the car, as he spoke these words to her:

"You are a prophet. You have a relationship with God that is different than those around you, but you will have to be alert, you will have to be ready no matter what comes at you. The people you will help, won't even understand how you got to them; TRUST GOD."

Just as suddenly as she was in the garden, she was back in the limo. Anthony was holding his hand out to her to help her from the car; they had made it to the office.

CHAPTER 4:
FAITH BUREAU OF
INVESTIGATIONS: F.B.I

Deuteronomy 18:15 (NKJV)
A New Prophet Like Moses
"The Lord your God will raise up for you
a Prophet like me from your midst, from
your brethren. Him you shall hear,

The building was massive; the doors were glass with champagne colored tint. On the outside of the building were the words B.A.D. LLC; this was the name of Damia's company in the states. Closing the car door and walking ahead of them Antonio spoke up about the name; "The instructions were to have a 'cover 'so that no one is aware of what goes on behind the scenes at the F.B.I. B.A.D LLC was given to us prior to your arrival." On the elevator, Antonio inserted a key into the lock on the keypad, and the elevator started to rise. He looked at them, and continued,

"I'm sorry that your travels here, and your training has been some what of a secret and has been strange to you, but it was necessary."

When the elevator door opened people started to applaud, and praise God. Damia was starting to feel full and excited; praising God herself as she walked on to the large floor full of cubicles, and copy machines. A bubbly woman walked up to her motioning to take her coat. Antonio spoke from behind them, "This is where you go on without me. I will be back at the end of your day. God bless you as you go forth in your assignments."

The bubbly woman took Damia's coat, as a young man was helping Anthony out of his. They both said in unison: "Welcome to your first day at *your* F.B.I."

"My name is Sabrina. I will be your secretary, Agent Willis."

"My name is Raul. I will be your assistant, Colonel Bishoff."

Anthony and Damia just smiled as they were led to one of the offices. They walked passed a large, cherry wood desk through gold double doors where Damia realized they were in her office. Pictures of her family and friends, books she had written, and awards she had received were throughout. The size of her office was larger than her living room in Milwaukee. At that very moment she was so humbled.

"Colonel Bishoff, your office is at the other end of the hall. I will take you there after your meeting," Raul stated.

"Meeting?" Anthony asked.

"Yes. We'll send him in." Raul and Sabrina walked out of the office. Anthony and Damia looked at each other like this cannot be real. Damia thinking of their two months of training never prepared them for the luxury they were experiencing.

A man in dark jeans, and white shirt, walked through the door with urgency; he was focusing on the file Anthony had in his hand. It was the same file that he was reading on the ride over.

"Have you gone over the entire file yet?" The man asked.

"Most of it," Anthony answered, "and you are?"

The man was walking towards a door north of Damia's desk when he answered Anthony, almost irritated by his question; "I'm Peter King. I'm here to help you get started today and today only. My assignment is to make sure you are comfortable enough to do what is necessary so that I don't have to come back tomorrow."

"Okay, but we've been through training," Anthony followed him through the door, to what seemed to be a private meeting room, "what do we need to know now?"

"The training you had been through was to get you adjusted to the change in your spiritual mindset and prepare you for all that you will see and do. Some government agencies give you book knowledge, then, expect you to do field work with a hit or miss attitude; you can't do that here." Looking at Damia, Peter reached his hand out to her, but Anthony stepped in front of him. "Colonel Bishoff, I understand your hesitancy. I understand your job to keep her safe. I am not here to harm either of you." He reached out again, took Damia's hand and started praying:

Father God, in the name of Jesus, we thank you for what you have done in Damia's life, we thank you that you sent her and Colonel Bishoff here to create this organization that will help saints prepare for the rapture. Lord we ask you to cover them as the go forth; we ask that you cover and prepare their staff daily. I ask you RIGHT NOW LORD that you give me the words to speak, to help them do this alone, but not alone. Give them both the strength they need to endure what they will see, hear, and experience. Father, I know that it is so in Jesus Name, Amen."

"Amen." Anthony and Damia said in unison.

Gesturing for them both to sit down, Peter pulled out files that had both their names on them. "Your training didn't prepare you for what you'll see in these files." As they opened them, Peter continued; "There is history in these files; your history. Agent Willis all those times God called you are in your file. Colonel Bishoff, all those times you worked and worked, trying not to hear God is in your file. Both of you have been wondering why Colonel Bishoff is here with you," Damia and Anthony looked at each and nodded, "He was the best choice to protect you. The dream you had that last week at work, Agent Willis, was God letting you know *ANTHONY* knew who you were, even if he didn't fully understand." Damia gasped. No one knew she had that dream. Now, they had an answer to why Anthony was here with her. "Colonel Bishoff's title and rank is higher than yours Agent Willis, but that is because we don't want outsiders to even know that you are the chosen one."

Again, Damia was light headed; she back at Minister Dallas' home; this time she was sitting at the dining table drinking tea.

"At times you may feel your strength waver, but you will have to endure, and stay prayerful. You will have intense dreams, and you will have waking visions. You will be challenged, and people will want to send you back to the states. You will be traveling to different places, and seeing things no one will ever see with their natural eye. You will be the eyes and ears for An-to-ny."

Her vision cleared and she was still in the office with Peter holding her hand. Looking at her intently, he spoke assuredly, "You will have those visions many times, Agent Willis. This is why you must always have a driver and some type of security detail." He let go of her hand, walked over to Anthony and silently prayed for him. "Colonel Bishoff, this is the new day of the rest of your life."

For the next hour, Peter went over their trainings and how it would help them daily. He gave them new Bibles, lists of contact numbers and addresses for staff.

By 3:00 pm lunch was brought in; the thought of sitting in this room for the remainder of the day was overwhelming to Damia. She looked at Anthony and wondered if he thought the same way.

Peter interrupted her thoughts saying, "The F.B.I. is your baby, Agent Willis. Faith Based Investigations. You will run it as God gives you to run. Your staff, including myself, is just here to assist you. There are prophets and overseers that may contact you with confirmation of what God has said, which is fine, but they can't tell you to go against what God has already told you to do. I know you're asking yourself, how do you help the people? What would they be contacting you about? Well," Peter slowed down some to allow the words to drip off his tongue and marinate in their minds, "The office will get notice of a situation happening, and make you aware of it-"

"And what am I supposed to do?" Damia asked.

"You will respond Biblically as much as you know how. See, right now, the transition that you are in is this, EVERYONE IS YOUR ASSIGNMENT NOW. The reason the F.B.I was established, and why you're the BOSS, sort of speak, is because you know how to be real, how to hear God, and how to lead. The truth is not a suggestion, it is the only option. The situations that will come across your desk will be the challenges people face that they can't explain. Things they have been through all along. "

"I'm confused," Anthony started, "Are we arresting, or helping? Are we shooting people or delivering them from curses and strongholds?" Peter and Damia were shocked by Anthony's question; neither expected him to sound so spiritual. "What? I'm asking, which, I don't think I asked during my training. There were things that have been embedded in my mind that I think should be answered.

"Let me ask you this, Colonel," Peter started, "What was your training like?"

"It was like being prepared for being a police officer. I did go to the shooting range, but I was also taught to fast and pray more. I was reading more of my Bible, and getting a better understanding. I was away from Damia and other people for 2 months. I had no other choice but to get connected, but am I truly?"

"Exactly, sir! You have to be ready for both sides of the spiritual spectrum, and NO, you are not truly ready, as Damia is not truly ready, but she is on a different level than you or I. Damia, I know that your training was more spiritual, but I also know that if you had to shoot a gun, you would. There will be some deliverance, and lots of prayer," Peter walked over to her and looked in her eyes so deep he was looking into her spirit and not at her flesh, "Damia, every bit of what you thought you knew will be challenged. You will have to go back and recall every vision, every dream, and every message God gave you. You're at the point right now, where you have to apply everything; God's word, His directions, and instructions. No more waiting on outside confirmation. You're IT sort of speak. "

Going back to the head of the table Peter continued with the insight of the F.B.I. "So, the paper work you were given the last weekend in Milwaukee, has more information on how all this applies to you and your growth over the next few months, but that's it. It really is all on you now Damia. You can always turn back, but with all you know right now you can't ever forget."

Peter looked at Damia waiting on some type of answer.

"What?" Damia looked right back at him with the same boldness he was emitting. "I'm not changing my mind," She looked over at her partner and new colonel, Anthony, "what about you?"

"I'm in." Anthony said without looking up from the papers in hand.

"Great." Peter gathered his items and started to leave. "I'm going to be available in the small office down the hall. It's between your offices. Once you get the hang of it, I'm out. I have to head back to Milwaukee."

"Back to Milwaukee?? You're from Milwaukee?" Damia asked, and Anthony looked up at Peter as well.

"I'm from all over. I was in Milwaukee watching over you for years. You will not understand right now, why, but eventually you will. I have to get back there because I have other assignments. I can't leave you two just yet."

"Watching over me?" Damia sat straight up in her chair, "What…"

"Later; get adjusted in your offices." With that, Peter walked out of Damia's conference room to his office.

"Watching you? How does he just leave on that note?" Anthony said as he, too, walked out of the conference room leaving Damia there to ponder what was just shared.

CHAPTER 5:
IN THE FIELD
TRAINING

Acts 17:11(NKJV)
*These were more fair-minded than those
in Thessalonica, in that they received the
word with all readiness, and searched the
Scriptures daily to find out whether these
things were so.*

Damia Willis had been running
since her phone rang two hours
ago.

*"Get to the office; your driver is
waiting!" Peter yelled in the
phone.*

*"What? What?" Damia was
talking to dead air. "Glad he didn't
use the video dial."*

*The car was waiting with Colonel
Bishoff inside. He never said hello,
he never looked up. Anthony
handed her a cup of coffee and said,
"We're in for it now."*

That's all she ran through her mind as she was chasing a man in black clothing, down a road into a brush and back into an area she knew nothing about. Damia could hear footsteps behind her that she knew were Anthony's. "Stop," She screamed, "F.B.I.! I said STOP!"

Anthony ran passed her with another agent in tow, and yelled, "Get back to the church. We'll take it from here." Damia noticed he had a gun in hand; it worried her that they may have to shoot someone.

She ran back to the church and had to face what she missed when she started running after the suspect.

What Damia was looking at now was beyond her; even in her creative mindset, this she couldn't fathom. She was looking at a woman that had been crucified outside a church in an area Damia was unfamiliar with. The woman was not only crucified but naked. The odd part about the crucifixition was there was no blood, and her eyes were closed. Damia asked herself, "Who would do this?" She started to turn away when she noticed that the woman was breathing; short and shallow, but breathing.

"Um, HELLO!!" looking around for help, Damia just started screaming at her team, "Hello, she's alive. Did anyone not know SHE WAS HANGING HERE ALIVE??? Get a med team here, ASAP!"

All of a sudden, people started running and making calls. Colonel Bischoff ran in and looked up at the woman, "We have to get her down."

"Did you catch the perpetrator? Did you catch him?"

"No," He said reaching up to try to get her down, "He disappeared in a wooded area; we just couldn't keep up."

"Stop, we don't know what we're doing; that's what the team is for. We are not equipped or trained in this area." Damia walked away from him and walked over to her driver who had conveniently stayed in the car. "Get Peter on the phone…"

"I'm here already, Agent Willis." Peter walked passed her over to the woman with four men walking behind him. "Get this woman down. The ambulance is on the way. Take her to the med room at headquarters."

"Headquarters? She needs a hospital." Damia barked at him.

Peter was in her face with three steps. With his height, he was towering over like a New York sky scraper. "Are you not connected with this yet? Is your mind on the assignment at hand? Look at this woman," Peter was in her face as if they were one. She could feel his breath on her forehead, "She's alive! At what point did you think this was normal? At what point did you forget??"

Gathering her wits, and holding back the urge to punch him Damia answered, "At the point where her life was on the line, that's where I forgot. I'm not ignorant of this; I'm just not used to it." Damia took a deep breathe, looked up at him with the same intensity that Peter looked at her, and spoke through her gritted teeth,

"Don't you ever snap on me like we're cool; you and I aren't there yet."

Peter smiled at her and whispered for only her to hear, "That's the Damia I want to see from now on. Don't hold back. God's got you. Remember, I've watched you for years. I know what you're capable of."

Anthony walked over, as they were taking the woman down from the cross, and asked Peter, "What is the story here? She was nailed to the cross, and no blood. Now, this is strange, but I think we're in for stranger."

"What's happening here Colonel is some type of religious act; something that, whoever put her up there felt would release this woman from any demons. This is what you call misrepresentation and understanding of the Bible."

Anthony looked at him and said, "What? She was hanging there with no bleeding? Explain that."

"I can't explain that! That's not my job; it's yours! Get on it you two!" With that, he got in the ambulance, "Wrap this up and get to the office!"

On the drive to the office, Damia was in deep thought. She was upset of how Peter spoke to her. It had been two days since the meeting with him in her office. She and Anthony were working on their new positions diligently going through papers and reading up on the different things that had happened in that they were unaware of

"You are not like the others." Minister Dallas stated.

"What others?" Damia said, realizing her voice was groggy.

"There were others before you; others I have tried to train. These were men and woman whom God had called, but we never went about choosing them as we have chosen you."

"I don't understand. Why does my head hurt?" Damia looked at Minister Dallas; he was disappearing before her eyes.

"We tried to train them in a controlled environment; not with you...." His voice drifted off.

Damia was back in the car; her driver was attempting to get her attention.

"How frequent are the visions?" Antonio asked.

"Not frequent at all. Yet."

"They will increase. Take it one day at a time. Your favorite tea is waiting for you in your office; it has been warmed." They got off the elevator amidst some hustle and bustle. As Damia headed to her office, her assistant was rushing out, and she heard Peter yelling.

"What do you mean you can't wake her up?? We need to figure out what has happened, and why." He walked away from the video phone in Damia's office as she was walking in the door. He walked passed her and closed the door on Antonio and ushered her into the conference room. "Look, I know you're mad at me for how I came to you out on the field, but some things are necessary..."

"Like you slamming the door in Antonio's face? He is my security..."

"Yes, like slamming the door."

"I'm wondering if I need security from you." She stopped in her tracks looking at Peter unsure of her safety.

"Are you for real?" Not waiting on an answer Peter continued, "Listen, I can't make you accept or feel comfortable with me, but I can say I have your best interest at heart. I KNOW, EXACTLY WHAT YOU ARE CAPABLE OF; I know you are stronger than you let yourself on to be." It was Peter's turn to pause; he looked at her with the same concern he had a few days ago. It was a look like a brother would have with a sister, when he knows he can't interfere.

Before Damia could counter him, Anthony and Antonio

walked through the door almost running.

"Okay, kids," Anthony started, "What's going on with waking up the crucified woman?"

Without missing a beat, Peter answered him, "Well, Colonel, the med team is saying they can't. I don't know if it is they can't RIGHT NOW, or that they just can't at all. What did you learn from the scene?"

Chiming in, Damia walked over to the video phone, "We learned that we're not equipped to run after perpetrators, we don't have what we need for fingerprinting, and I don't carry a gun." She dialed the number to the med floor to speak to the team about their progress.

"Good morning Agent Willis..." Dr. Miller started.

"It's afternoon, and I'm tired. Can you bring me up to par with what is happening, with….with our Jane Doe?"

"Well, we have her name," He walked of his desk and retrieved a printout, "Her finger prints were in an international database which is odd…"

"Her name Dr. Miller; what is her name?"

"Her name is Sheba Michel. Before you ask, Agent Willis, we haven't investigated her life to find any family information. We're still searching."

"Get back to me, Dr. Miller as soon as you find out more…"

"Dr. Miller, what about waking her up?" Anthony interrupted.

"Colonel, we have tried everything this side of slapping her, and nothing has worked, but we're still trying."

"Try harder," Peter and Anthony said at the same time, "We need to move on this investigation."

Antonio had reheated Damia's tea and was handing it her as he whispered in her ear, "More challenges are yet to come, Agent Willis, be encouraged." As she looked up to say thank you, he was walking swiftly out the door.

CHAPTER 6
IT'S ALL SPIRITUAL

Amos 3:7(NKJV)
7 Surely the Lord GOD does nothing,
Unless He reveals His secret to His
servants the prophets.

Two weeks after the crucifixion
of the woman, the F.B.I. wasn't
any closer in waking her or
finding the perpetrator. Many
leads came in but never panned
out.

It was the weekend, and Damia
had just gotten off the phone
with Prophetess Tavia Kennets;
it had been months since they
had spoken. Damia was
flipping through channels on
the television when she was
back in the garden with
Minister Dallas.

She was walking through six feet tall rose bushes of various, vibrant colors.

"Well, well, Damia, it has been a while. How are you?" Minister Dallas, came out of nowhere, and walked passed her.

"I'm sorry, what?" Damia turned to him and he gestured for her to sit down on a white bench.

"OH yes. You haven't gotten fully attuned to what is happening to you. These visions you keep having."

"No sir, I don't." She was starting to feel light headed.

"Let me get you some tea, Damia. Tell me what you have experienced since your training." Minister Dallas, walked away, and retuned just as quickly with a crystal tea cup.

"The investigation we're working is hitting a dead end. I can't understand why we can't wake the woman up."

"Do you realize she's royalty?" He looked out towards the rose bushes, and continued without a beat, "Roses come in various colors. They are beautiful, and vibrant, but the stems have thorns. Pain in beauty." He looked at her and asked again, "Do you realize she's royalty?"

"No, sir, I didn't and I'm lost about how the roses and Sheba Michel connect." Sipping on the tea, she felt better.

"You have to realize, Damia, that everything is spiritual..."

"Don't use me against me. I know that everything is spiritual, Minister Dallas."

"Then why is this so hard?" He got up and started walking down the path in the rose garden, "Come with me."

As they started walking along the path in the rose garden, Damia noticed how cohesive the color patterns of the roses were; how they just flowed from one color to the next to the next.

"Each color of the rose has its own meaning, both spiritually and naturally. Significantly it reminds us of love; Sheba's name means promise. She was crucified because she's a reminder of a promise, like the rose reminds us of a love."

"I don't get it." Damia said. Minister Dallas folded her arm in his as she swayed a little. Almost immediately on the other side of her was a beautiful woman who held on to her other arm. She had a look of concern on her face.

"This is too MUCH FOR HER L.A.!"

"Damia, you remember my wife Debra?" They came to another white bench in the garden, where they sat her down; Minister Dallas' wife still had a look of concern. She had retrieved Damia's tea, which was helping, but she was still worried.

"Damia, how do you feel? What do you see?

"You're both fading somewhat, and my head is starting to hurt, but the tea is helping."

"L.A. end this, she's not strong enough."

Minister Dallas knelt down in front of her handing her a folded piece of paper, "Damia, everything is spiritual. This will help you in your investigation, but I want to see you again. Not like this; not in a double reality. I want you to have your driver call me when you awake in the morning. There are so *many probabilities and possibilities to your life…"*

"L.A!!!" Mrs. Dallas yelled.

"What are probabilities?" Damia asked, but everything was starting to fade; she dropped the crystal tea cup. "What?"

"Damia, this paper will help you. Remember…"

They both faded away; Damia was back in her room in her apartment with the remote still in her hand. No time had passed since she had 'gone'.

As she got up to get something to eat, her hand landed on a folded piece of paper of by her pillow. The paper smelled of roses; it was the paper Minister Dallas had given her in the garden.

She unfolded the paper, and recognized the picture of Sheba

Michel. It was the personal information Damia and her staffed couldn't find. It also contained some information that would explain why she was crucified.

"But why won't she wake up?" Damia thought out loud.

About the Author

Dana Neal was born and raised in Milwaukee, WI. She is a wife, mother, and CEO (Christian Encouragement Officer) for many business and organizations.

Dana Neal started writing in elementary, and high school, where she wrote short stories in her spare time and poetry for her schoolmates.

Damia Willis, F.B.I. is Dana's first fiction character; starring in three books under the same title.

"This is an exciting achievement for me, even though I have been writing for years; decades. I thank God that He gave me the gift of being a Prophetic Scribe, but also the mind and wisdom to see what He's saying. With Damia Willis, you have to determine, as the reader, is it really fiction. I want to personally thank Alba Henderson, and Shamico Winger for their encouragement in writing this book."

Dana Neal
www.ckqllc.biz/CF.html
info@ckqllc.biz